THE
MAGICAL
TRUNK

A BOOK OF COLORS

WELCOME
TO FIRST GRADE

This book is being given to you
by the
**Bridgeport Public Education Fund
and SVA**

through the generosity of
Fleet Boston Financial
Fairfield Women's Exchange, Inc.
Ruth I. Krauss Estate
Near & Far Aid Association
Southern Connecticut Gas Company

This book belongs to

_____

The Magical Trunk
A Book of Colors

Written and
Illustrated
by

GiGi
Tegge

Greene Bark Press
P.O. Box 1108
Bridgeport, Connecticut 06601

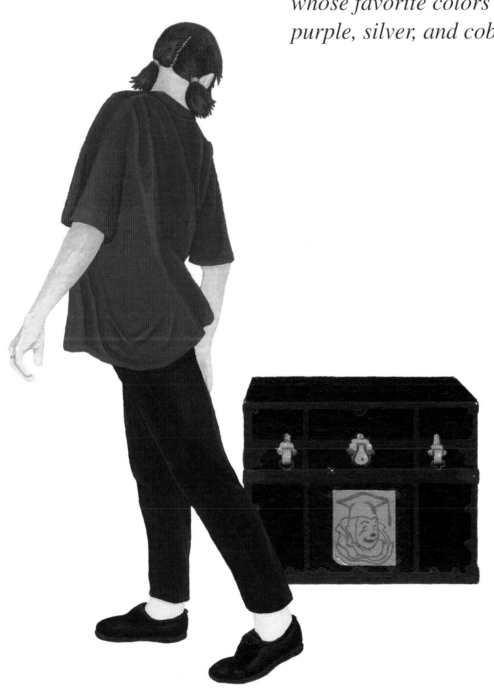

*For Edina, Frank, and Lizehte,
whose favorite colors are
purple, silver, and cobalt blue.*

Publisher's Cataloging-in-Publication
(Provided by Quality Books, Inc.)
Tegge, Gigi
     The magical trunk : a book of colors / Gigi Tegge. --
1st ed.

     p. cm.
     SUMMARY: Gentle and colorful exploration of a clown's
trunk containing make-up and magic.
     Audience: Grades K through 3.
     LCCN 2001134141
     ISBN 1-88085-167-9

     1. Colors--Juvenile fiction. 2. Clowns--Juvenile
fiction. 3. Colors--Fiction. 4. Clowns--Fiction.
I. Title.

PZ7.T2275Ma 2001   [E]
                QBI01-700792

I was walking along, one gray day, when I came across a trunk.
"Ho hum," I said. "Just an ordinary trunk."
But when I opened it wide,
I found something very different inside.

"Wow!" I said, "Zip, Zowie, and Gadzooks!"
Because, of course, that is what you say
When you find a magical trunk.

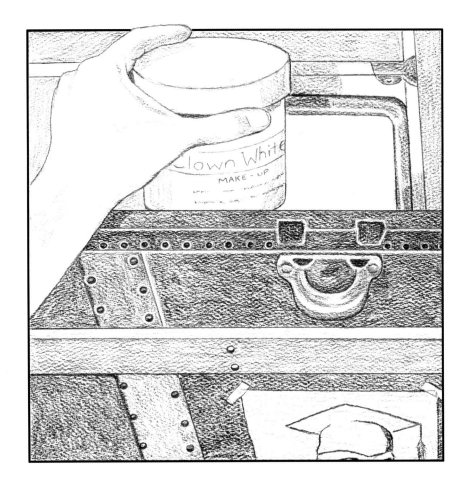

I found a jar of white in the magical trunk,
A big tub of ooey-gooey white.
And when I spread it on my cheek--
Eek!
Something white began to happen...

RED

I found a tin of red in the magical trunk,
A thin tin of icky-sticky red.
And when I tapped some on my nose--
Whoa!
Something red began to happen...

BLACK

I found a tin of black in the magical trunk,
A small tin of greasy-gluey black.
And as I painted carefully--
Yippee!
Something black began to happen...

PINK

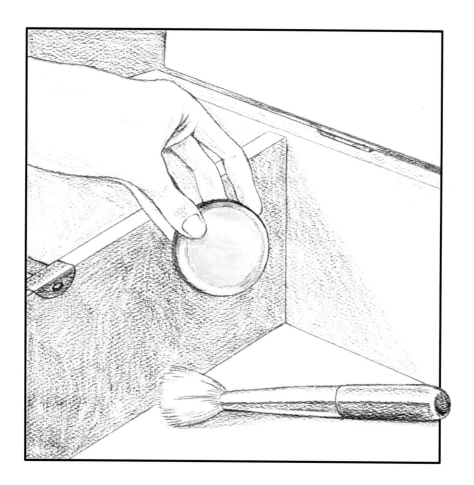

I found a bit of pink in the magical trunk,
A tiny tin of powdery pink.
Yes, when I put some over my eye--
Me oh my!
Something pink began to happen...

YELLOW

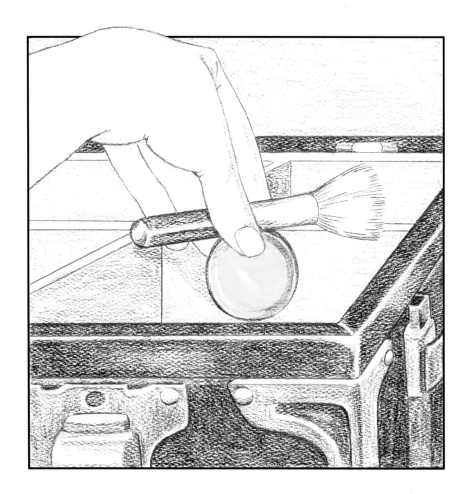

I found a bit of yellow in the magical trunk,
A small bit of sunny-honey yellow.
Oh, when I brushed it on my brow--
Wow!
Something yellow began to happen...

ORANGE

I found a wig of orange in the magical trunk,
A fuzzy-furry bundle of orange hair.
Well, when I put it on my head just so--
Presto!
Something orange began to happen...

GREEN

I found a ruffle of green in the magical trunk,
A wrinkly-crinkly clown's ruffle.
When I stretched my neck and pulled it round--
Zounds!
Something green began to happen...

PURPLE

I found a hat of purple in the magical trunk,
A teeny-tiny top hat.
And when I placed it right on top--
Pop!
Something purple began to happen...

GOLD

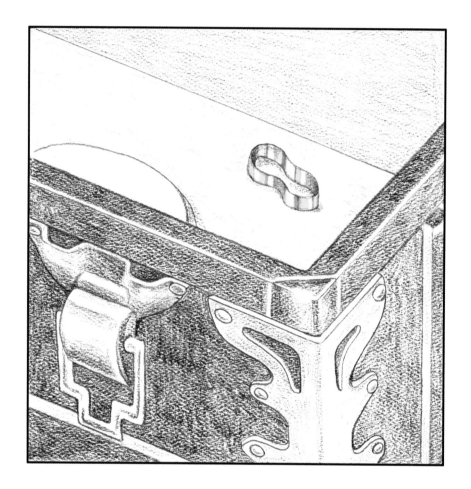

I found a band of gold in the magical trunk,
A sparkly-twinkly hatband.
Of course, when I slid it on my hat--
Look at that!
Something gold began to happen...

SILVER

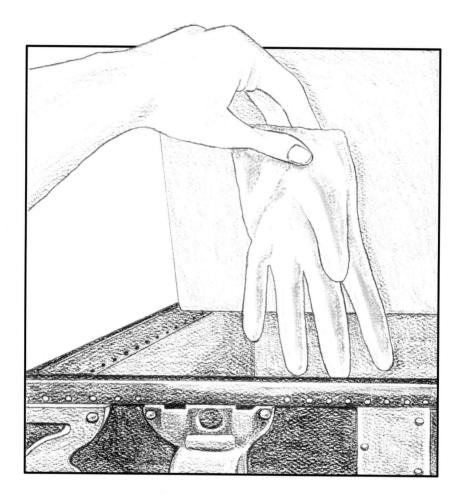

I found two gloves of silver in the magical trunk,
Two shimmery-shiny gloves.
And when I pulled on one and then two--
Yahoo!
Something silver began to happen...

BROWN

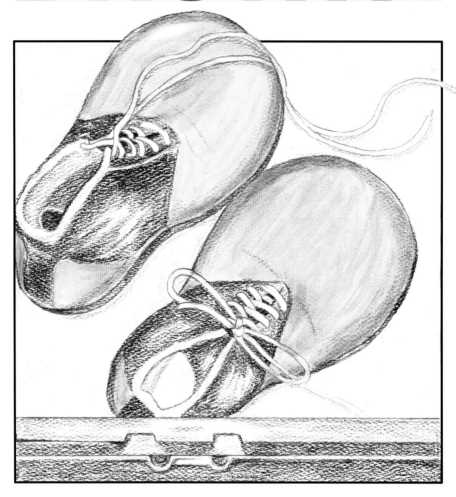

I found two shoes of brown in the magical trunk,
Two big shoes for my two small feet.
Yes, when I slipped in just one toe--
Kablam-o!
Something brown began to happen.

BLUE

Then, at the bottom of the magical trunk, I found a paper of blue,
An invitation just for me!
And when I gave it to the blue clown,
At the blue curtain,
Peeking out of the blue tent,

EVERYTHING began to happen...

Bright things of white, red, black, pink, yellow,

orange, green, purple, gold, silver, brown, and blue!

So, if you're walking along, some gray day,
And you happen upon the magical trunk,
Go ahead and open it.
Because if you do--
Woo-hoo!

Something
White,
Red, black
Pink, yellow, orange,
Green, purple, gold, silver, brown, and blue...

May just happen to you,
Too.